MIRACLE MOMENTS IN TENNIS

KENNY ABDO

Fly!
An Imprint of Abdo Zoom
abdobooks.com

abdobooks.com

Published by Abdo Zoom, a division of ABDO, P.O. Box 398166, Minneapolis, Minnesota 55439.

Printed in the United States of America, North Mankato, Minnesota.
052021
092021

THIS BOOK CONTAINS RECYCLED MATERIALS

Photo Credits: AP Images, Granger Collection, Icon Sportswire, iStock, Newscom, Shutterstock
Production Contributors: Kenny Abdo, Jennie Forsberg, Grace Hansen
Design Contributors: Dorothy Toth, Neil Klinepier

Library of Congress Control Number: 2020919506

Publisher's Cataloging-in-Publication Data

Names: Abdo, Kenny, author.
Title: Miracle moments in tennis / by Kenny Abdo
Description: Minneapolis, Minnesota : Abdo Zoom, 2022 | Series: Miracles in sports | Includes online resources and index.
Identifiers: ISBN 9781098223236 (lib. bdg.) | ISBN 9781098223939 (ebook) | ISBN 9781098224288 (Read-to-Me ebook)
Subjects: LCSH: Tennis--History--Juvenile literature. | Tennis--Records--Juvenile literature. | Sports--History--Juvenile literature. | Miracles--Juvenile literature. | Curiosities and wonders--Juvenile literature.
Classification: DDC 796.342--dc23

TABLE OF CONENTS

TENNIS

Even with so many other sports in the world, tennis is still considered an **ace** among them.

It is believed that tennis came from northern France in the 12th or 13th century. Then, a ball was hit with the palm of a hand. Major Walton Clopton Wingfield wrote the rules and patented the game in 1874.

Everything from record-setting match lengths to hard-fought victories have graced the clay court.

DO YOU BELIEVE?

Bjorn Borg shocked the world at the 1980 **Wimbledon Championships**. Up against infamous John McEnroe, Borg won the **title** with a final backhand pass. It was a tie-break win that has become tennis legend.

During the 1985 **Wimbledon Championships**, unknown 17-year-old German Boris Becker beat all-star Kevin Curren. Becker was the youngest player to ever win the tournament. He said, "This is going to change tennis in Germany." And it did.

Ending 2006 at number 95 in the world, Serena Williams was down and out. Making it to the 2007 **Australian Open Grand Slam** finals, Williams stunned by taking down number one player Maria Sharapova. It is considered one of the finest Grand Slam performances of all time.

The 2010 **Wimbledon Grand Slam** saw John Isner and Nicholas Mahut play the longest-ever tennis match to date.

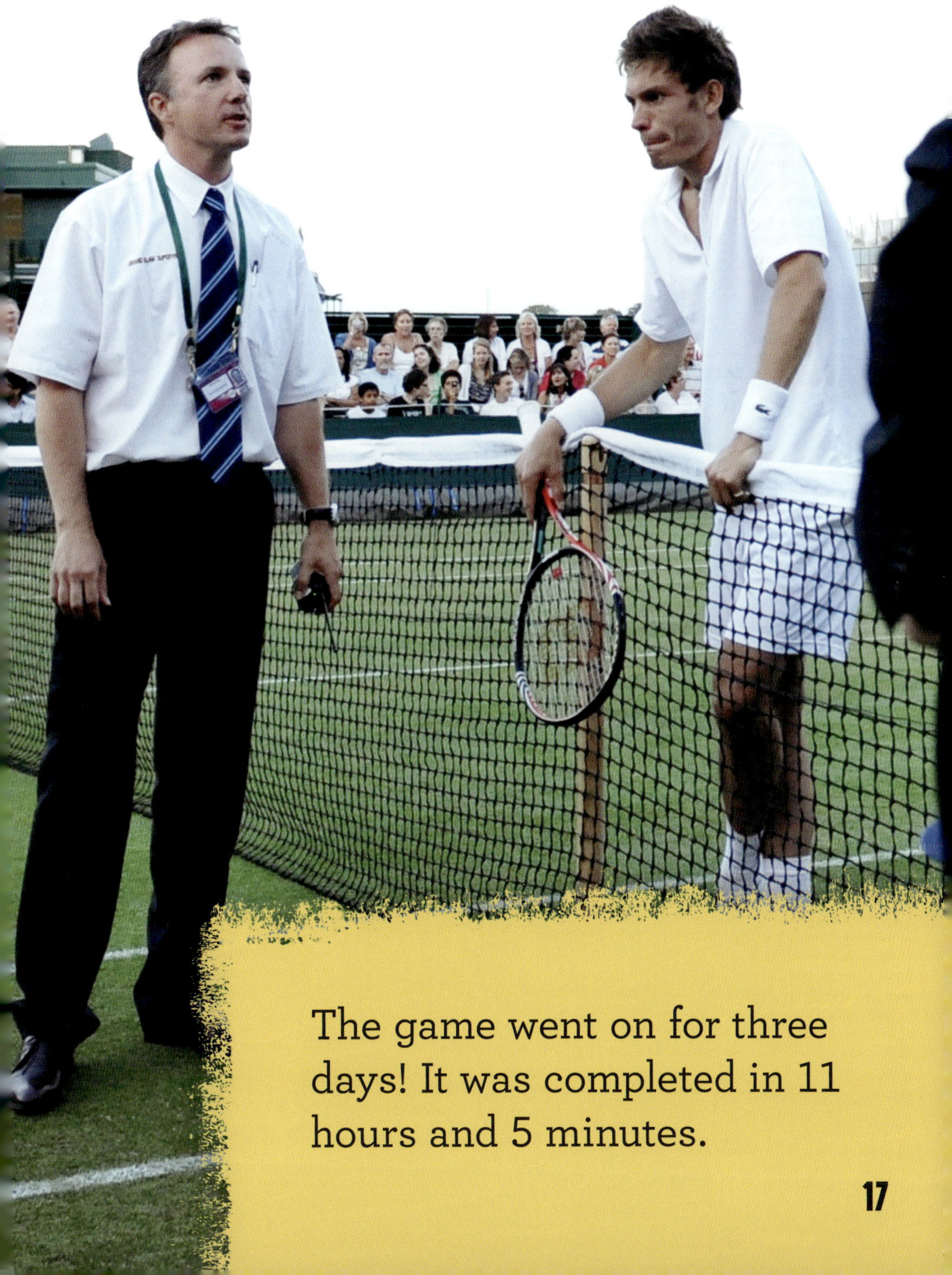

The game went on for three days! It was completed in 11 hours and 5 minutes.

Andy Murray made history at **Wimbledon** in 2013. He became the first British player to win since 1936. He was also the first Scotland born person to win a singles **title** since 1896!

ROYAL MARSDEN
adidas
adidas

LEGACY

These tennis court miracles have been captured in time. Not with just **highlight reels** and books, but with movies and documentaries.

Tennis has dedicated athletes and fans who all agree that with this sport, "love" means more than just zero.

GLOSSARY

ace – a winning serve that the returner does not touch.

Australian Open – the first of the four most important yearly tennis tournaments.

Grand Slam – also known as the majors, are four of the most important yearly tennis events, which includes the US, Australian, and French Opens and Wimbledon Championship.

highlight reel – the best moments of a certain game or athlete compiled into one film.

title – a first-place position in a contest.

Wimbledon Championship – the oldest and most respected tennis tournament in the world.

ONLINE RESOURCES

Booklinks
NONFICTION NETWORK
FREE! ONLINE NONFICTION RESOURCES

To learn more about miracle moments in tennis, please visit **abdobooklinks.com** or scan this QR code. These links are routinely monitored and updated to provide the most current information available.

INDEX